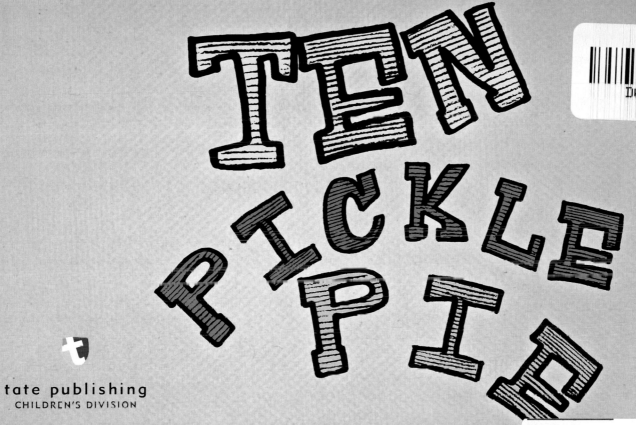

TEN PICKLE PIE

tate publishing
CHILDREN'S DIVISION

Chris Garrison

Published by Tate Publishing & Enterprises, L
127 E. Trade Center Terrace | Mustang, Oklah
1.888.361.9473 | www.tatepublishing.com

Tate Publishing is committed to excellence in
the philosophy established by the founders, bas

Book design copyright © 2013 by Tate Publish
Cover and interior design by James Mensidor
Illustrations by Greg White

Published in the United States of America

ISBN: 978-1-62510-071-9
1. Juvenile Fiction / Imagination & Play
2. Juvenile Fiction / Cooking & Food
13.09.02

I like breakfast, lunch, and dinner,
Ice cream in the summer, and soup in the winter.

But my favorite dish, any time of year,
is one I'm sure your taste buds will fear.

It's a pie of sorts, common enough.
That is, until you add the right stuff.

There's flour and sugar, cinnamon too.
Butter and salt, with eggs beat to a goo.

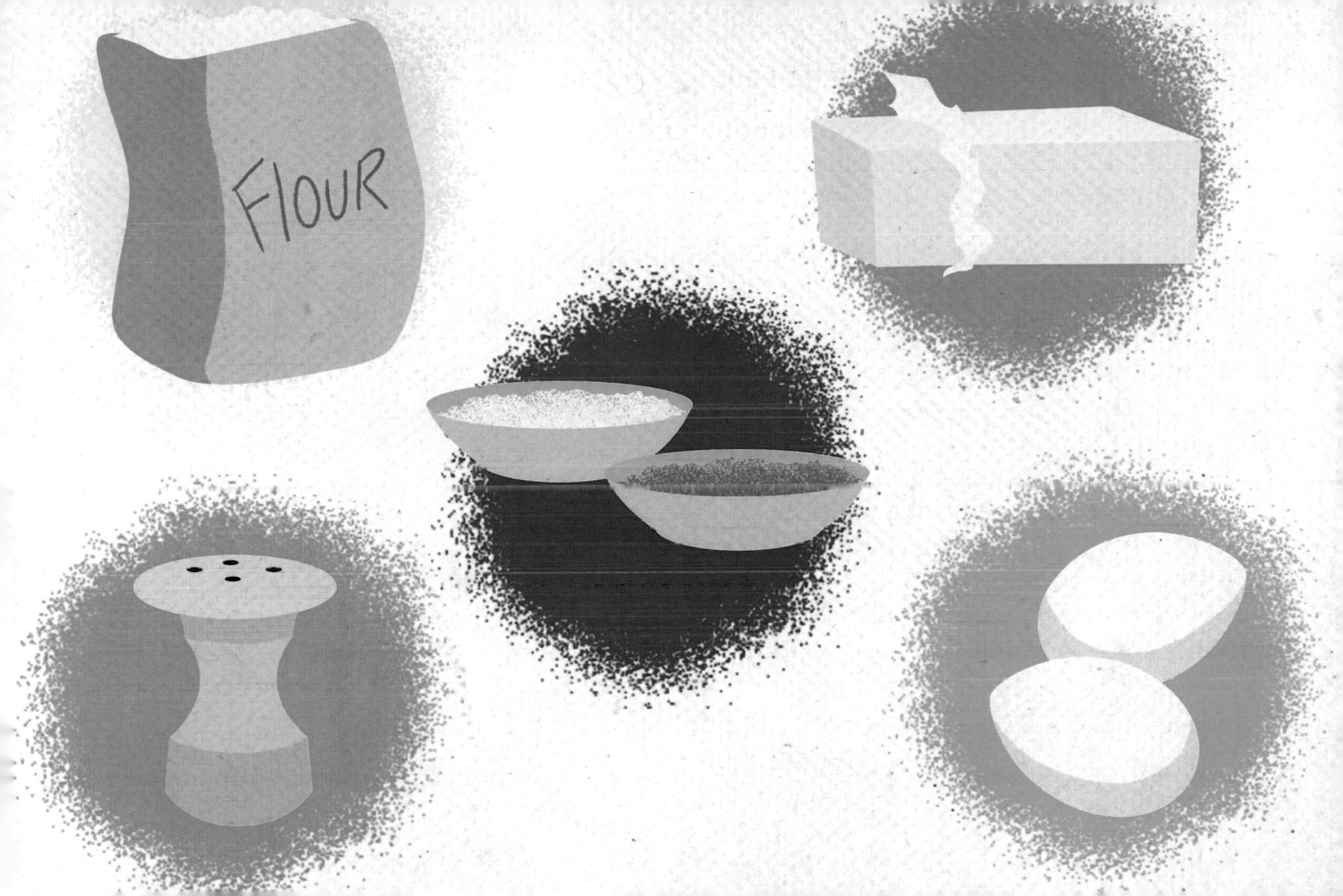
FLOUR

But my secret ingredient is the reason why I,
call my kitchen creation ten pickle pie.

It calls for ten pickles, plump and sour,
diced into chunks then baked for an hour.

Enjoy it still hot with ice cream on the side,
and take your taste buds on an unexpected ride.

The crust is so crisp, crunchy, and flakey.
The pickles are sour, salty and tangy.

So kids of all ages, ask your parents for help.

Warm up the oven, but not by yourself.

Gather the ingredients and pile them up high,
then you too can enjoy a slice of ten pickle pie.

e|LIVE

listen|imagine|view|experience

AUDIO BOOK DOWNLOAD INCLUDED WITH THIS BOOK!

In your hands you hold a complete digital entertainment package. In addition to the paper version, you receive a free download of the audio version of this book. Simply use the code listed below when visiting our website. Once downloaded to your computer, you can listen to the book through your computer's speakers, burn it to an audio CD or save the file to your portable music device (such as Apple's popular iPod) and listen on the go!

How to get your free audio book digital download:

1. Visit www.tatepublishing.com and click on the e|LIVE logo on the home page.
2. Enter the following coupon code:
   2548-3319-bf75-7d4a-4436-8926-061d-1f2b
3. Download the audio book from your e|LIVE digital locker and begin enjoying your new digital entertainment package today!